ARTHUR LOSES A FRIEND

差点少了一个好朋友

（美）马克·布朗　绘著

范晓星　译

CHISO 新疆青少年出版社

Today was the last day
of school for Buster.
Tomorrow he was going
to his dad's for a month.

"Have fun, Buster," said Mr. Ratburn.

"But don't forget your homework."

Arthur went to the airport
to see Buster off.
"It's going to be great
to spend a whole month
with my dad," said Buster.

4

"I'll miss you," said Arthur.

"Don't worry," said Buster.

"I'll send lots of postcards."

Then he waved good-bye

and got on the plane.

The next day,

Arthur ran home from school.

"Any mail from Buster?"

he asked his mom.

"No," she said.

"He just left yesterday,"

said D.W.

7

Every day, Arthur looked
in the mailbox.
But there was nothing
from Buster.

Two weeks passed
and still not a word.
"Maybe Buster broke his arm
and can't write," thought Arthur.

Arthur called Buster's mom.

"How is Buster?"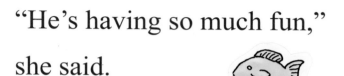

he asked her.

"He's having so much fun,"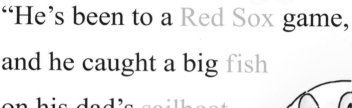

she said.

"He's been to a Red Sox game,

and he caught a big fish

on his dad's sailboat.

He's even made some friends.

He plays football with them."

"Oh," said Arthur.

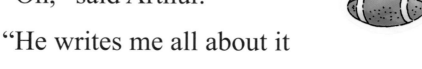

"He writes me all about it

in his letters and postcards,"

said Buster's mom.

That night, Arthur said,
"I think Buster has forgotten
all about me."
"Have you written to him?"
Arthur's dad asked.

Arthur got a pen and paper.

He wrote:

 Dear Buster,

Why haven't you written to me?

Your friend,

Arthur

The next day at school,

Arthur said to Francine,

"I just sent Buster a letter."

"I just got a letter from him,"

she said. "He's having fun."

"Buster's having so much fun,"
said Arthur to the Brain.
"Sounds like he has forgotten us."
The Brain held up a postcard.
"He didn't forget me,"
said the Brain.

Days passed.

At the dinner table,

Arthur played with his peas.

He didn't even finish

his bowl of strawberries.

"Can you believe it?" he said.

"Everyone has heard

from Buster but me."

"Don't worry," said his mom.

"You'll see him in two days."

"Don't be sad, Arthur,"
said D.W.
"You've got lots of friends."
"But Buster was my best friend,"
he said.

Arthur hugged Pal.

"You're my best friend now,"

he said. "But I wish

you could tell funny jokes

like Buster."

The next day, the mailman
called to Arthur,
"I have a lot of mail for you."
And he pulled out of his sack
ten postcards and three letters.

"Mrs. Hammer brought them
to the post office this morning,"
said the mailman. "She said,
'Stop bringing me these.
There is no Arthur
at 265 Main Street,
where I live.'
But I knew that there IS an Arthur
at 562 Main Street."

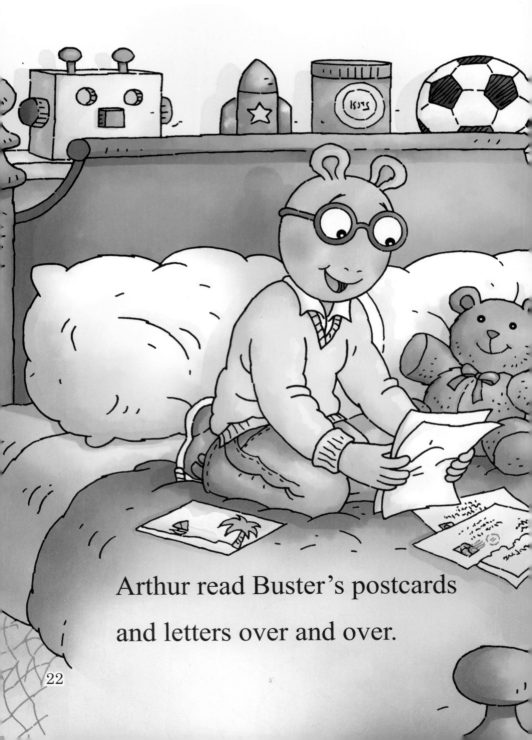

Arthur read Buster's postcards
and letters over and over.

"I'm having lots of fun,
but I really miss you,"
wrote Buster.
"This month with my dad
was really great,
but it will be great
to come home, too,"
he wrote in another letter.

Buster called Arthur

as soon as he got home.

"Can I come over?" he asked.

Arthur laughed.

"Sure, if you can find my house!"

译文

2. 今天是巴斯特最后一天来学校。

明天，他要到爸爸家去住一个月。

3. "祝你开心，巴斯特！"舒老师说，"可别忘了做作业！"

4. 亚瑟去机场为巴斯特送行。

"和我爸爸住上一个月一定非常好玩。"巴斯特说。

5. "我会想你的。"亚瑟说。

"放心，"巴斯特回应，"我会给你寄很多明信片。"说完，他挥挥手，走上了飞机。

6. 第二天一放学，亚瑟就飞奔回家。

"巴斯特给我来信了吗？"他问妈妈。

7. "没有呀。"妈妈回答。

"他不是昨天才走的吗？"朵拉说。

8. 每天，亚瑟都会去看看邮箱，可惜巴斯特什么都没有寄来。

9. 两个星期过去了，还是没有一封信。

"也许巴斯特的胳膊骨折了不能写字。"亚瑟想。

10. 亚瑟给巴斯特的妈妈打电话。

"巴斯特怎么样？"他问。

"他过得可开心了，"巴斯特的妈妈回答，"他看了红袜队棒球比赛，还坐他爸爸的船钓到一条大鱼。

11. 他还交了好几个新朋友，每天都和新朋友们一起踢足球。"

"哦。"亚瑟回应。

"他写信、寄明信片告诉我这些事的。"巴斯特的妈妈又说。

12. 晚上，亚瑟说："我觉得巴斯特一定把我忘了。"

"你给他写信了吗？"爸爸问。

13. 亚瑟拿来笔和纸，动手写起来：

"亲爱的巴斯特，你为什么没有给我写信呢？你的好朋友，亚瑟。"

14. 第二天上学，亚瑟对芳馨说：

"我刚给巴斯特写了一封信。"

"我刚收到他寄来的一封信，"芳馨回应，"他过得很开心。"

15. "巴斯特玩得太开心了，"亚瑟对小灵通说，"好像把我们大家都忘了。"

小灵通拿出一张明信片说："他没有忘记我呀。"

16. 又过了好几天，晚饭的时候，亚瑟没精打采地拨弄着豌豆。他连自己那碗草莓都没有吃完。

17. "你们相信吗？"亚瑟说，"每个人都收到巴斯特的信了，只有我没收到。"

"别担心，"妈妈安慰他，"再过两天你就能见到巴斯特了。"

18. "别难过，哥哥，"朵拉也说，"你有很多朋友呢。"

"可巴斯特是我最好的朋友啊！"亚瑟嘟囔。

19. 亚瑟抱抱宝儿，说："现在你是我最好的朋友了，可是我多想你也会讲逗人的笑话啊，就像巴斯特那样。"

20. 第二天，邮递员叔叔来找亚瑟说："我有很多信要给你呢。"说着就从邮包里掏出十张明信片和三封信来。

21. "韩太太今天上午把它们送到邮局来的，"邮递员叔叔说，"她还叮嘱说，'别再送错信了，我住的梅恩大街 265 号没有叫亚瑟的人'。幸好我知道，梅恩大街 562 号住着一个叫亚瑟的小孩儿。"

22. 亚瑟把巴斯特的信和明信片读了一遍又一遍。

23. "我过得可开心了，不过我真的很想你。"巴斯特写道。

"我和我爸爸度过了特别棒的一个月，不过回家的感觉一定也很棒。"在另一封信里巴斯特这样说。

24. 巴斯特一回到家就给亚瑟打来电话。

"我能去你家玩儿吗？"他问。

亚瑟笑着回答："当然，只要你能找到我们家在哪儿！"

ARTHUR LOST in the MUSEUM

亚瑟的博物馆体验

（美）马克·布朗　绘著

范晓星　译

CHISO 新疆青少年出版社

The bus stopped at the museum.

Arthur's class got off.

Arthur started to run

up the steps.

"Stop!" shouted Mr. Ratburn.

"You must all stay with me.

I don't want anyone

getting lost."

3

"Today we will visit
the Hall of America,"
said Mr. Ratburn.

Arthur raised his hand.

"Save your question, Arthur,
until we get there,"
said his teacher.

"Now follow me, boys and girls."

They walked by
the Hall of Dinosaurs.

Arthur raised his hand again.

"No, Arthur, we do not have time
for the dinosaurs today,"
said Mr. Ratburn.

"That's not what I wanted to ask,"
mumbled Arthur.

But his teacher just kept walking.

"Here we are," said Mr. Ratburn.

"The rooms in here

tell the story of our country.

You'll see how Indians lived

before the Pilgrims came,"

he said.

Arthur raised his hand again.

"Okay, Arthur," said Mr. Ratburn.

"What is your question?"

"May I go to the bathroom?"

Arthur asked.

Everyone laughed.

"Yes, Arthur," said Mr. Ratburn.
"The boys' room is around
the corner.
It's the first door on your left."

Arthur ran down the hall.

He turned the corner

and went into the first door—

on the right.

"It sure is dark in here,"
said Arthur to himself.
He saw another door.
"Maybe the toilets are in here,"
he said.

He opened the door
and stepped into a room
filled with Indians
sitting by a tepee.
"Help!" he screamed.

Then he saw that the Indians
were not alive.

They were models.

One wall was glass.

And there was Mr. Ratburn
telling his class about the Indians.

But no one was listening to him.

They were all laughing
and pointing at Arthur
with the Indians.

14

AMERICAN
INDIANS

15

"I'm in big trouble," said Arthur,

"if I don't get out of here fast."

He ran out the door

and left the Indians behind him.

"What's so funny?"
asked Mr. Ratburn.
He turned around and
saw only Indians making baskets
and arrows.

Arthur crept along the dark hall
to the next door.
"I sure hope
this is the boys' bathroom,"
he sighed.

But it wasn't a bathroom.

It was a room showing

the Pilgrims' first Thanksgiving.

And Arthur's teacher was telling
his class all about it.
Everyone laughed
when they saw Arthur.
Mr. Ratburn turned to see
what they were laughing at.
But not before Arthur
became a Pilgrim boy.

21

When Mr. Ratburn's class left,
Arthur took off the Pilgrim hat.
"I've got to go NOW!" he said.
He left in a hurry.

He ran down the dark hall…

and he found the boys' room—
just in time!

Arthur found his class
by a room with
George Washington.
"What took you so long, Arthur?"
asked Mr. Ratburn.
"I was making history,"
said Arthur.

2. 校车在博物馆前停稳，同学们挨个从车上走下来。

亚瑟飞快地跑上了台阶。

3. "等一下！"舒老师大声喊，"大家一定要跟着老师走，我可不希望有谁走丢！"

4. "今天咱们要重点参观的是美国历史展厅。"舒老师说。

亚瑟举起手来。

"等一下再提问，亚瑟，我们进去再说。"舒老师说，"现在，大家跟我进去吧。"

6. 他们从恐龙展厅经过。

亚瑟又举起手来。

"不行，亚瑟，我们今天可没时间看恐龙。"舒老师说。

"我不是想说这个。"亚瑟小声嘀咕。

可惜舒老师只顾朝前走。

26

8. "就是这儿了，"舒老师说，"这间展厅展示了我们国家的历史，大家可以看到印第安人在欧洲清教徒到来之前是怎样生活的。"

亚瑟又举起手来。

"好吧，亚瑟，"舒老师说，"你有什么问题？"

"我可以去卫生间吗？"亚瑟问。

孩子们哄堂大笑。

10. "可以，亚瑟，"舒老师回答，"男卫生间在拐角那边，左手第一个门。"

11. 亚瑟跑过大厅，转过拐角，走进了第一个门——右手那个。

12. "这里面可真黑呀！"亚瑟自言自语地说。

他又看到了另一扇门，心想："这里可能是卫生间。"

13. 亚瑟推开门走进房间，看见一些印第安人坐在帐篷旁边。

"救命啊！"亚瑟大喊。

14. 很快，亚瑟就发现那些印第安人不是真的。

它们只不过是一些人物模型。

这个房间有一面墙是玻璃的，舒老师正在外面给同学们讲解印第安人的历史，可惜谁都没听他说什么，每个同学都指着印第安人的模型和亚瑟笑得前仰后合。

16. "我得赶紧离开这里，不然就麻烦了。"亚瑟对自己说，他飞快地跑出门，离开了那些印第安人模型。

17. "什么事那么好笑？"舒老师问。

他转过身，只看见正在编篮子和做箭头的印第安人模型。

18. 亚瑟在走廊里摸黑朝前走，走到又一扇门前。
他自言自语地说："但愿这一定是卫生间。"

19. 可惜这也不是卫生间，里面展现的是欧洲清教徒们在美洲大陆度过第一个感恩节时的情景。

20. 舒老师正在外面给其他同学讲解这一时期的历史。
同学们看见亚瑟，又哄笑起来。
舒老师转过身去看大家到底在笑什么，可惜亚瑟已经假扮成一个清教徒小孩儿了。

22. 直到舒老师和同学们都走开了，亚瑟才摘下清教徒的帽子。

"我得赶紧离开这儿！"他边说边慌慌张张地跑了出去。

23. 他沿着漆黑的走廊往前跑……总算找到了卫生间——好险呀！

24. 亚瑟在介绍乔治·华盛顿的展览橱窗前找到了舒老师和同学们。

"亚瑟，你怎么去了那么久？"舒老师问。

"我呀，亲自去历史场景里逛了一圈！"亚瑟回答。